Pet
School
Day

ReadZone Books Limited

50 Godfrey Avenue
Twickenham
TW2 7PF
UK

First published in this edition 2014

© in this edition ReadZone Books Limited 2014
© in text Hilary Robinson 2005
© in illustrations Tim Archbold 2005

Hilary Robinson has asserted her right under the Copyright Designs
and Patents Act 1988 to be identified as the author of this work.

Tim Archbold has asserted his right under the Copyright Designs
and Patents Act 1988 to be identified as the illustrator of this work.

Every attempt has been made by the Publisher to secure appropriate
permissions for material reproduced in this book. If there has been any
oversight we will be happy to rectify the situation in future editions or
reprints. Written submissions should be made to the Publisher.

British Library Cataloguing in Publication Data (CIP) is available
for this title.

Printed in Malta by Melita Press

ISBN 978 1 78322 471 5

Visit our website: www.readzonebooks.com

Pet to School Day

by Hilary Robinson
illustrated by Tim Archbold

READZONE

"Today is pet day,"
said Mr Spink.

"Where's your pet, sir?"

"At home. He's too wild."

"Is he a bull?"

9

"Is he an elephant?"

11

"No," said Mr Spink.
"My pet is a…

…dinosaur!"

14

"Have you had him for thousands of years?"

"I caught him on Sunday.
He wears a red collar, eats
trees and drinks from the bath."

"Where can you catch dinosaurs?"
"In a dinosaur park."

"How?"
"With a dinosaur net,"
replied Mr Spink.

21

"Can anyone do that?"

"Only with a permit," said
Mr Spink.
"When you catch a dinosaur
you get a badge like mine."

"How can you get a permit?"
asked James.

"You have to show that you are a brave dinosaur warrior," said Mr Spink.

"You're not!"

"How do you know I'm not?"
asked Mr Spink.

"Because you're scared of
spiders and," said James,
"to prove it, this is…

Max!"

Did you enjoy this book?

Look out for more *Magpies* titles –
fun stories in 150 words

The Clumsy Cow by Julia Moffat and Lisa Williams
ISBN 978 1 78322 157 8

The Disappearing Cheese by Paul Harrison and Ruth Rivers
ISBN 978 1 78322 470 8

Flying South by Alan Durant and Kath Lucas
ISBN 978 1 78322 410 4

Fred and Finn by Madeline Goodey and Mike Gordon
ISBN 978 1 78322 411 1

Growl! by Vivian French and Tim Archbold
ISBN 978 1 78322 412 8

I wish I was an Alien by Vivian French and Lisa Williams
ISBN 978 1 78322 413 5

Lovely, lovely Pirate Gold by Scoular Anderson
ISBN 978 1 78322 206 3

Pet to School Day by Hilary Robinson and Tim Archbold
ISBN 978 1 78322 471 5

Tall Tilly by Jillian Powell and Tim Archbold
ISBN 978 1 78322 414 2

Terry the Flying Turtle by Anna Wilson and Mike Gordon
ISBN 978 1 78322 415 9

Too Small by Kay Woodward and Deborah van de Leijgraaf
ISBN 978 1 78322 156 1

Turn off the Telly by Charlie Gardner and Barbara Nascimbeni
ISBN 978 1 78322 158 5